UNLEARNING

Breaking Free From Tradition and Societal Norms

Raheen R. Frith

UNLEARNING. Copyright © 2024. Raheen R. Frith. All Rights Reserved.

Printed in the United States of America.

No portion of this book may be reproduced, stored in a retrieval system, or transmitted in any form or by any means, except for brief quotations in printed reviews, without the prior written permission of DayeLight Publishers or Raheen R. Frith.

ISBN: 978-1-958443-75-0 (paperback)

ACKNOWLEDGMENTS

To my parents, Barbara and Winston Frith, your love, guidance, and belief in me have been the cornerstone of my journey. Your love for each other taught me to love others and never stop trying and believing in them. Thank you for being my constant inspiration and for instilling in me the belief that there are no limits to what I can achieve.

I am grateful to my family and friends for their support, encouragement and presence in my life. Your belief in me and your steadfast support through every triumph and challenge has meant more to me than words can convey.

I am indebted to life itself for the countless lessons it has taught me. Every experience, whether joyful or painful, has contributed to shaping the person I am today. I am grateful for the opportunity to grow and evolve and for the wisdom gained along the way.

This book is a testament to the journey of self-discovery and the pursuit of individuality. It is the reflection of the lessons learned and the transformative power to unlearn. I am humbled by the opportunity to share insights with others in the hopes that they too may find empowerment and enlightenment on their own paths.

To all who have contributed to this journey, whether through words of encouragement or simply being a presence in my life, I offer my deepest gratitude. Your belief in me and this work made it possible for me to share this gift with the world.

With heartfelt appreciation,

Raheen

TABLE OF CONTENTS

Acknowledgments iii
Introduction: What Does Unlearning Mean To Me? 7
Chapter One: Embrace the Fear: Finding Courage in Uncertainty 11
Chapter Two: Navigating Life Without Organized Religion 29
Chapter Three: Cultivating a Culture of Acceptance 39
Chapter Four: Navigating Life on Your Own Terms 47
Chapter Five: Thriving Into the Unknown 53
About the Author 61

INTRODUCTION

WHAT DOES UNLEARNING MEAN TO ME?

Unlearning is a process. There are three stages to this process. These three stages require me first to recognize habits that no longer add value to my life or bring good results. Secondly, I would need to slowly release these things by becoming open to change and prepared to feel uncomfortable as I take gentle steps out of my comfort zone. Lastly, I replace the things that have yet to work with solutions I have discovered or contemplated, knowing they will work out for me. Even if it is not the best solution, I keep going because, in the end, I have to figure out what works for me by gaining knowledge and finding my best fit in life, which aligns not only with my purpose but with who I am.

I have been feeling tired, frustrated, overwhelmed, disappointed, confused, and annoyed since early January 2021. Working from home as a freelance graphic designer did no justice to my financial stability and only made me question the purpose of my work. I was tired of seeing, at most, JA$100 in my bank account. Yet, people genuinely believed I was living it up with a decent amount of money in my bank account. I am independent and seek to maintain this mindset at all times. So, several times, I declined offers to go out with my friends because I didn't have enough money. However, my kind-hearted friends didn't usually ask if I had money; instead, they told me to get ready and urged me not to worry about the money. While I can be very vocal about my struggles, whether financially, emotionally, or mentally, I choose whom I vent to with caution to protect my space and control the ammunition people have over me if we ever 'fall out.'

Every year, I go to New York for work, but the plane tickets can be pretty expensive. I prefer to wait and save for the trip beforehand instead of rushing or borrowing to leave for New York. This year, with the busy season already underway and the first dime yet to be found, the trip seemed unlikely. Then, serendipitously, an old friend contacted me about a job offer in a new city!

Initially, I was unsettled about the opportunity, given the unfamiliarity of everything. However, my biggest concern was the promised hourly wage. Hearing the proposed amount would scare most people, and it seemed like a genuine waste. I kept making excuses and barely tried to secure the job, but my friend's enthusiasm was contagious. He assured me that gratuities significantly boosted overall earnings, as it had sent him through college twice to get his degrees. After hearing his stories, I finally decided to try it, even if I would do it scared. There is a valuable lesson to learn from this experience, and I am eager to share the full story with you. I don't know about you, but the prospect of earning an income in US currency fills me with excitement and inspires me to work nonstop! Call it motivation if you must.

CHAPTER ONE

EMBRACE THE FEAR: FINDING COURAGE IN UNCERTAINTY

Many times, if you want to obtain meaningful and authentic results from what you do, you must do something out of your comfort zone. You will never know if something works for you if you never try it. Similarly, you might try a friend's solution, which doesn't work for you but works for them, which is entirely okay; this only proves that we may go through similar situations but have completely different paths, suffering, and goals. Suffering usually carries negative connotations, but there is potential for good to come from it, even if we fail to accept it initially. Of course, everything is not always what it seems. However, we must learn to make a bold move to test how far we are willing to go to make our dreams a reality. This will, by necessity, demand our focus, smarts, and keenness in our decisions.

When I tell you that not everything is about money, I mean it. Some connections and experiences are worth more than any amount you could get in your bank account. Imagine seeing something you can never afford; all you can do is wish. It is painful and, often, paralyzing. I promise you, often, the issue is not that people don't want to work; they lack the opportunity and/or experience. For instance, in Jamaica, your experience is of little significance in some cases because the hiring managers believe you can only handle the workload if you have a certain amount of subjects or a particular degree. Conversely, I can be job hunting for months and never get a call back because I am not qualified enough. I would talk about the opportunities that have presented themselves over the past year, but this book seeks to capture my journey since moving to Wyoming from April to October 2021.

I have never been ashamed of the job that pays my bills, but unfortunately, some people's priorities are out of line. How can you be ashamed of what puts a roof over your head and food in your kitchen? My friend who invited me to Wyoming understood the struggle in Jamaica and knew that what I was earning from freelance graphic designing wasn't enough for a steady income or survival. I was only comfortable because my parents didn't pressure me to buy anything or pay any bills. Regardless, I helped when I could, even without them asking me. I would feel quite uncomfortable being there without contributing where I could; I would effectively be back at square one and reliving the feeling I spoke about in my first book, "UNLOCK: The Journey to Purpose." It pushed me to accept the offer to work in Wyoming because it was better than doing nothing or earning insufficiently. I thrive on ensuring my parents and family are well cared for; that makes me happy. I will continue to put them first because they continue to go above and beyond to ensure I am happy and comfortable.

It was my first time being in the United States without family nearby. My sister stayed in New York, but I was miles away from her in Wyoming. What I looked forward to the most was having my own apartment. I was unfamiliar with anything outside of staying with my parents and my sister, so the experience opened my eyes to what I could be doing a few years from now: God's will.

When I arrived in Wyoming, I focused like never before. I had goals and a vision, which I will share with you in a few moments. For now, I will take you on a journey, step by step, so that you can understand the value of determination.

I devoted my time to working crazy hours without a day off because I believed I could make it work, and guess what? I did! But only for a month. I started working from 8 a.m. to 2 p.m. and then transitioned to the 11 a.m. to 10 p.m. shift. Eventually, it took a toll on my body. I was in constant pain, and the more I complained to my friends and family, especially my mom, the more they impressed on me that no amount of money was worth it. I caved. I took a break from working a whole month without a day off to prioritize my mental health and do the things I love the most, including dancing and catching up with my family and friends. I needed it! That day did so much for me, and I was ready to take on the week. A few months later, I started looking for a new job; strangely, I wasn't particularly motivated to complete the applications. I knew I wanted the job, but I hesitated. I don't believe I was procrastinating because I knew I wanted the job to make some extra money. Additionally, when I leave Jamaica to work elsewhere, I leave with the mindset that I left for work and not pleasure.

I worked as a server at a restaurant; this was my first time in the industry, so everything was new to me. I had never heard of or encountered these things in Jamaica or when I travelled otherwise. Naturally, I was overwhelmed with all the new information I needed to learn in training before I could start serving tables. I also had to bartend for a few days with one goal: ensuring the customers had a great experience. I made so many mistakes along the way, which put a lot of pressure on me. I am grateful for my friend and the manager I had because, even when I messed up, they reminded me that it would be okay. They encouraged me to give myself time, but being the perfectionist I am, this was challenging. This journey, though, was a teacher. I learned that I was somewhat impatient to go through certain processes to learn the right way. I also realized there are no shortcuts to your destiny or what was meant for you. You should, consequently, take as much time as you need to learn and give yourself some credit for trying because it all starts with you. As cliché as it sounds, we all need a reminder that we must be our biggest motivation. I forgot this at one point, so it took me so long to settle down. Understanding life and your process will teach you that there is so much more to learning than just learning to do the work instead of learning to do the work and make a change while at it.

Serving in the restaurant has taught me a lot. I have built numerous connections since I have been there, many of which I did not imagine building, including those with complete strangers. Each time I was assigned a table to serve, I had two intentions: serving them and building a great professional relationship with them. No, it is not weird to ask a customer about their profession based on the conversation that may occur. I have seen instances where customers ask me about my country of origin because they heard my accent. They also understand that people come to work at that particular location from all over the world.

This is how we build a connection with people and start great conversations. You never know who you are serving at a table. They may be authors, entrepreneurs or business owners with multimillion-dollar businesses. I have gotten job offers from customers because of how I treat them. I am often amazed by how others see in me the things I don't see in myself. This is primarily because I am still discovering myself and working on my flaws. Surprisingly, people from that small town seemed very understanding. I kept telling everyone I had never been anywhere like that before and would never trade that experience for anything.

Of course, just like everywhere you go to live or work, nothing is perfect, but as long as you stay out of the drama and mind your business, I assure you, you will be fine wherever you go. I treat people how I want to be treated, and there is no way to escape your genuine character and personality when you do that.

UNLEARNING

I needed to leave Jamaica and be on my own for a while; the most significant thing that happened to me was my unlearning phase. It was so scary and weird for me, but I got through it because I realized that most of the things I learned growing up were what others taught me. There was very little about what I learned for myself, though many people may not accept this.

As it relates to church, I have let go of so much; however, I remain in God's arms because I know that nothing and no one could have brought me the joy or achievements that have been inundating me over the past months.

As a reader of this book, you may already be familiar with me through social media or word of mouth, and you know I am a dancer. My journey began with liturgical dance in my church, and I have since expanded my repertoire to include Afrobeat, minus the versions containing vulgarity or anything derogatory. My love and passion for dance has intensified! I can't allow a day to pass without taking at least 30 seconds to dance, no matter the pain I may be feeling. I have decided to dedicate more time and energy to the things that promote calmness and bring peace to my mental health. No one truly understands the depth of happiness and freedom I feel when I dance. When I hear a beat and start to move my feet and sway my arms, the rhythm keeps me alive. Going forward, I intend to take my dance career more seriously because there is so much I can learn and even teach from it.

I am in the process of unlearning so many things, including my connection to God. Many people might perceive my current path as that of a backslider, but I have been doing everything possible to maintain my new lifestyle and connection with God. I built this connection solely on our relationship. It doesn't have to look like what people want it to be. Still, I am sure I have been much better, freer, and at peace with my faith. It is about knowing my limits and knowing that I can do what I love while I remain a vessel that can be poured into—so long as I open my ears and mind with a willingness to learn and accept changes.

I know many youths who have reverted to their old lifestyle because they feel pressured; the sense of stagnation despite their efforts to transform their lives and live for God can become overwhelming. Now, more than ever, mental health struggles are becoming increasingly prevalent, leaving many struggling to find solid ground on which to stand. They are bombarded with so many different perspectives on how to live and what to do but barely take the time to catch up on freeing their minds from the mental prisons they face. Constantly battling the struggles, they have been told to let go, or they will not see God's face. When they desperately cry out for help, no one is willing to listen to the most sensitive parts of their story because people are fixated on abstinence or shortcomings, leaving little room for genuine conversations. There is no time to speak about the harsh realities we face as youths. I was in that number. Thankfully, I found solace in writing and had the chance to talk to people I trust, people in my space or community facing the same issues. The more I do this, the more confident I feel in fighting for my mental health and what I need to do to evolve as a man.

Recognizing the need for change in our lives can be one of the most challenging things to do. Why? Familiarity creates a sense of comfort but makes it hard to see beyond what we have known for years. Unlearning can be very long and difficult, but being determined is one of the most powerful things you can ever do for yourself. While unlearning, be very careful of your choices. Avoid rebellion as best as possible. Be honest with yourself; if you don't think you can handle the journey by yourself, don't hesitate to seek help from someone who can guide you properly. A life coach or therapist can be valuable on this journey. Evolution does not require a journey along the path of rebellion.

I remember the constant happenings while I was in Wyoming; it was a whirlwind, causing me to feel more successful than ever. I had almost forgotten that God's hand was still at work even when it wasn't apparent. It can lead to a sense of disconnection from God when our prayer life is weakened or we feel far from God. However, even in the unseen moments, God is always there, guiding us to make the right choice. In my last book, I spoke about rebellion and how it can significantly delay your purpose. Be cautious; take your time and ensure you are making the right choice.

I experienced living alone for six months, which included taking on the full responsibilities of adulthood. I had become addicted to independence and making money to enjoy life. I sacrificed so much to survive, to ensure that I would be independent of my parents upon my return to Jamaica. I have never worked so hard in my life, and I couldn't be more proud. Initially, giving myself credit for my accomplishments was hard, but that kept me humble. However, I realized I worked harder when I acknowledged my hard work in making my long-held dreams a reality. It doesn't make you 'full of yourself' to be proud of yourself and your accomplishments.

I know it can be difficult to step outside of the walls of your comfort zone, but to grow, that is precisely how it should be. Learn to get uncomfortable to grow into who you are supposed to become. Enjoy the moment you are living in, but remember, time waits on no man; every second counts. Do what you love and enjoy; make sure you live not just for the moment but according to your purpose as aligned with everything you know God has called you to do.

If you have been following me on social media, you will know I am very vocal and unashamed of my faith. I let the world know I am saved, and God is my number one priority. The only thing I never do is push God down someone's throat, especially young people. My goal is to empower those I am called to lead, guiding them toward a comfortable, happy, and purpose-driven life by integrating their passions with purpose and service to God.

UNLEARNING

The line gets a little blurry when we believe God has to change His will to suit our lifestyle. As much as we wish it were so, He never changes and will never force us to do something we do not want to do. It is all about choices. Let me be very honest with you: it can be very easy to doubt that God can do something you asked for instead of remembering the many things He did for you when you didn't see it happening for yourself. Please do not lose sight of your vision or run from the great work you have already started. If your purpose or vision feels overwhelming, take a break, reassess, and find your balance. You were not built to help everyone; do enough for those you are called to support and take care of your mental health.

Working as a restaurant server taught me humility. I learned the importance of apologizing, willingly acknowledging my flaws, and finding solutions readily so I can move on to my next guest. It is something I would never trade, and I would do it all over again because the lessons learned are lifelong treasures. The people I met changed my perspectives, how I saw others, and my approach to situations.

I met a lady at the resort where I was working in Wyoming; she was frequently misunderstood by many people. We built a fantastic relationship while I was there. It seemed farfetched because, initially, I believed we were complete opposites. It was hard for us to find common ground because we weren't listening to each other. In the beginning, many people were trash-talking about this coworker, telling me to stay away from her because of their experiences with her.

Being the person I am, I wouldn't want someone to believe what strangers say about me without getting to know me first. So, I decided to ignore the negativity and took the time to work with her and understand her personality. Sometimes, the negativity almost got to me because it seemed my effort was going nowhere. But I stuck with it, and then, something happened that rocked her world. She didn't trust anyone else, so she confided in me. She believed she could speak to me without her secrets being published to the entire city. From that moment, I could see her heart. All she ever wanted was for someone to listen to her without judgment. We started talking more, and eventually, I decided to confide in her.

She reminds me of my mom; she is very hardworking, but the problem with Izzi is that she never takes a break. She worked seven days a week, fifteen hours or more daily; I had to do my utmost to talk her out of it because her body needed rest, and I could tell she was drained. Eventually, she listened; today, she is one of my closest friends.

It is a daily reminder to get to know people for yourself and, in the same vein, know GOD for yourself. Build your own relationship with Him, not based on someone else's faith or how others want you to know Him. Open your ears and understand that at the end of the day, there is always a reason or a lesson to be learned in every phase of your life.

I made so many errors while I was at the restaurant, but I always made it known that I was willing to take full responsibility for them. Therefore, no one could say I did or didn't do something if I disagreed, and I was happy my boss saw this side of me. Live according to your heart and vision, but most importantly, live according to your purpose. Put actions to your words and watch everything manifest. The goal should never be just to want something, but it should also consider making the effort to get it. Make as many sacrifices as you need for that dream to come alive, and I promise you the joy you will feel from it cannot be bought.

We need people— even when we feel like they have failed us way too many times for us to ever put an ounce of trust in them. Some people would never give you the time of day or opportunity, even if they had it at their fingertips to give to you so you can grow. Fortunately, my friend saw it fit for me to win and make money with him; he called me and helped me. If I had been prideful, I would have stayed in Jamaica, struggling to make ends meet while trying to grow my business. Though things were moving slowly, my stay in Wyoming made that vision one step closer to what I needed my business and youth organization to be. Fully empowered, I began to pursue my plans actively. I could give back as generously as I wanted because God had allowed even strangers to pour into me. For instance, God instructed me to bless a few people with a hundred dollars (US$100) or a minimum of fifty dollars (US$50), and it came back to me.

I remember walking to work one afternoon to start my shift, and as I was about to enter the building, a gentleman appeared suddenly and said, "Hi, are you going in to start your shift now?" I told him yes. He then reached into his pocket and pulled out a $100 bill. He told me he was 'just following orders' and that I must have a great day, make more gratuity, and not just let it end there for the day. I was a bit puzzled by his actions since we were strangers at the time. Later that day, he revisited the resort and came to the pub section where I was serving. I was urged to ask him what he meant when he said he was following orders. I wondered if it was time for me to take both my feet in my hands and run for my life. Was someone watching me? My mind raced. Remember earlier I told you that conversing with guests was normal to get to know them? Yes, so it wasn't weird when I later asked him what he meant by following orders. Based on the conversation that developed, he spoke like a man of faith. So, I asked him if he was saved (a Christian), and he said yes! It was a huge relief! Now I knew that it was God who allowed him to do that because earlier that week, I had sent One Hundred United States Dollars to someone God told me to bless. While the recipient didn't understand it since it was unexpected, I told the individual not to mention it.

Following divine instructions will allow people to do unexpected things. My publisher always tells me that it is not always about the money but more about the life-changing impact your story can have on the people you reach. I held on to that, and every time I served a table that changed my day for the better or forged a great connection, I gifted them a copy of my book. Their excitement always created a scene which left me feeling quite shy the whole time. Despite this, these interactions helped me to build some amazing connections. These people have supported me nonstop, and I appreciate them so much.

Over those months, I learned to be bold and more outspoken than ever before. I became more mature and accountable. Not everyone will understand the sacrifices you make to secure your future and dreams, but that is okay. It is not for them to understand. Those who need to see the vision –will. They will work with it even when you become unavailable to the point where you can no longer communicate or socialize as you did previously. It is okay to disappear and go off the grid until you have settled yourself and your priorities. Those who are offended by how hard you work do not need to be involved in your journey to a better life. Let people come and go as they want, but make sure you set boundaries.

A coworker unintentionally taught me a profound lesson about how people saw me. I overheard her telling someone that I was too nice. She saw me as someone who wouldn't speak up if someone did something I didn't like; she said I did nothing but laughed it off. Her advice to the person was not to be like me in that regard. That experience transformed my personality, causing me to become more assertive in my speech and actions. I commanded respect in my interactions with people; being laid back is fine, but you cannot be too easy. It is important to establish boundaries, or people will mistreat you at will. Likewise, know that if your independence threatens someone, it is because they don't have the opportunity to control you.

Be content with what you have until you get your overflow. An opportunity awaits you when you least expect it, but it will only come to you if you are willing to work for it. It doesn't matter how much you pray; if you don't decide to change or cause something to shift, everything will remain the same. Cherish your experiences and learn from every moment, whether present or future.

Well, my life took a turn, didn't it? This book is proof that everything is unpredictable; you never know, even when you have solid plans and visions. To those who knew me, I was a devout church attendee, attending as frequently as five days per week. That changed when my vision of what my journey was like and should be became more apparent to me. In the past, when people shared their bad experiences with the church, my first question focused on their errors and why they dealt with the issue in the way they did. Now, I wish I could take it all back because, having gone through certain things, I can understand the pain, anger, and resentment so many people went through and are still going through. I locked away certain emotions, believing I was wrong to feel them. Now, I realize those things kept me from digging deep into what I truly needed to do to evolve and reach my full potential.

Now for a challenge. What are two things you are most indecisive about now in your life? Think about why you feel

UNLEARNING

uncertain. Take a few minutes and not just think about what you can do to change being uncertain but write it down, and within the next 2-3 weeks, challenge yourself to have an open mindset about how you can change the perception and change how you have always seen your situation. Each time you have an idea how you can do this, come back to this section and write it down and any solutions you found so the future you—the stronger and more confident you—can remember how and when you started becoming the better version of yourself.

CHAPTER TWO

NAVIGATING LIFE WITHOUT ORGANIZED RELIGION

The thing I dislike the most about religion and denomination is the segregation that comes with it. After sharing a part of this new version of myself on my social media platforms through a video series, I was alarmed to hear the many horror stories, some from persons I did not expect, who had gone through so much but never talked about it. It wasn't that they didn't want to speak about the struggles; they did, but they were also afraid of being ridiculed. They didn't want to be labeled as needing deliverance. The truth is that deliverance isn't always the answer. While not all churches push that idea, it has become widespread for people to feel insecure and afraid to talk, ask questions or feel a particular emotion because they don't want to be labeled and put on the *back bench*. I have seen it and been through it myself. Sometimes, if you dare to ask a question for clarity, you are whipped with, "Don't you dare question the leader or the Word of God." If we are honest, we will read some things in the Bible that our human sensibilities would prefer to reject. For instance, the biblical concept of turning the other cheek. Many of us would like

UNLEARNING

to react and take revenge, right? Admittedly, not everyone is like this because we all think differently. However, the evidence is clear; we are not limited to thinking any one thing or questioning things. There is nothing wrong with wanting answers. Certain churches employ methods of correction that are demonstrably wrong and inhumane.

One experience left an indelible mark on me, a memory forever etched in my mind. I was at a church where I previously served during convocation nights. I can vividly recall the phase I was going through, including my struggle with depression and personal life issues. A guest pastor was visiting, and though we never spoke before that night, it seemed he had a problem with me for some unknown reason. He previously preached at certain fasting and deliverance services, which I often attended, and as soon as I entered the building, his message changed to something completely different.

One night during the convention, the visiting pastor did something I never saw coming or thought someone in their right mind would ever do. He put me on blast, humiliating me in a way that defied reason. I thought it came from God, but I was so naïve. However, I am grateful for the experience; now, it would never happen the way it did. He called me forward before the entire congregation. His voice boomed over the microphone as he declared that young men who spend too much time around women are gay and in need of "deliverance." He launched into a story and ranted on about how he felt about homosexuality. He spoke in tongues and over the microphone, which anyone at least a mile from us could hear; he laid his hands on me and preached deliverance. I glared at him the entire time because while I was embarrassed at how he weaponized his *'preaching'* and *'prayer'* for me, an angry question arose in my mind. Where was he when I desperately needed help and prayers to pull me out of the web of depression and suicidal thoughts of wanting to do more and be more of what others said I should be?

That experience caused me to struggle with my image of pastors afterward. After embarrassing you and putting you on the *back bench*, they called it correction and then have the audacity to say that God never destroys a city without warning—the hypocrisy. My world and so many things around me changed. For those who are familiar with Jamaica's culture, the eventual backlash after that night wasn't surprising; it didn't matter whether it was true or not. The fact that the word came from someone highly respected, whose ministry was said to be powerful, would naturally cause people to believe it, take it and run with it. So they did. It baffles me how some people classify public humiliation as 'open rebuke' and agree with it, failing to consider the impact on the recipient's life.

Bitter and inconsiderate; that is all. Did it hurt me? Yes. Did it change how I saw the church's approach to biblical interpretation? Yes. But did it make me bitter? No. Despite people's mistakes, we can see their approach, lifestyle, and treatment of others without allowing it to change how we see the world and those in it. This generation does this too much; consequently, it has become the norm to bleed on everyone who comes after our storms, perpetuating the myth that the good suffers for the bad. I do not believe in revenge, but life has a way of teaching lessons to us when we hurt people with pure hearts and intentions. We must be careful about how we treat others in platonic and romantic relationships. Kindness and genuine love for one another never fail.

About one to two years later, the guest pastor confronted his own storm; he received backlash, public humiliation or what some would call 'exposure.' Allegedly, this was because he mishandled certain situations, and his prophecies were said to be inaccurate. My storm revealed a major societal problem: we underestimate the value of good communication. We fail to grasp the weight it carries. If it is done correctly, countless errors can be avoided. Regardless, I now shield my heart from certain situations; I have learnt acceptance, and as a result, I now allow things to flow as they are destined to and see things objectively for what they are.

Sharing my experiences in church sparked a wave of gratitude; many people reached out to me, thanking me for voicing the unspoken questions and feelings since they didn't have the courage to speak aloud about the things they were feeling or ask the questions for which they needed answers. I reminded them that asking questions and seeking answers was a strength, not a weakness. I assured them—they will not always lack boldness; they need only to experience the transformative truth of God and their humanity.

Many live based on beliefs instilled in their youth; their past dictates what is right versus wrong. This does not mean that everything you learned was wrong; still, everything is not right either. We cannot live our lives based solely on the norms and traditions of our past. I cannot stress enough how all our journeys differ; even if the destination is the same, we all take different routes, and there is no one to tell us we are wrong.

Living in someone's shadow, believing they have the key to life, is an easy recipe for destruction. We must make our own mistakes and navigate them ourselves. Remember, **there is no shame in learning; that is the source of our strength.** I have seen how denominations come between churches; segregation is always heartbreaking. People have their personal beliefs, vision, and way of doing things. Often, it has nothing to do with what the Bible says but how they think things should be done, usually based on personal preferences and tradition. Some people are unbothered by women processing their hair and wearing makeup and pants; others are against it. I have been thinking, and I realize that there are few boundaries concerning women since the church emphasizes grooming them to become wives and to avoid fornication. There is less focus on grooming men to become husbands and leaders and on counselling them regarding their mental health. There is so much that men must learn on their own, usually the hard way. I am grateful for the few conferences and workshops now being hosted specifically for men. These are positive steps towards providing valuable skills and guidance for men.

Our lives shouldn't be centered only around the church; we need a life outside of it while maintaining a relationship with Christ. I remember the first time I said that to some of the most seasoned Christians I knew; they told me I needed deliverance. It chilled me. It delayed me from getting to where I am now. I felt like I was being controlled and manipulated. I didn't want to go against the Bible, and this thought drained me because I always felt like I was 'in the wrong.' Getting a job for myself offered no comfort to me because I would constantly hear "wait."

When I asked, "Wait on what?" I was told not to question God. But how can I not question something that improves my life and takes me out of certain struggles? I heard that I was being a rebel and that I never listened. Sometimes, I was sure I knew myself and why I reacted the way I did. But for some reason, I was always 'in the wrong' because I was too young to understand. I used to know when I did something wrong, even when I didn't want to admit it, because of pride. I still do. Maturity allowed me to apologize then and now, holding myself accountable for what I did. Why? I cannot live with guilt. Even when I attended church regularly and frequently heard of the importance of knowing God for myself, I didn't understand it until I came out of the church space for a while. Just because we don't attend church five days a week doesn't mean we love God less or are drifting;

we can still maintain a pure lifestyle and relationship with Him outside of the building and services. Some people worship, praise, and pray better this way because they don't feel the pressure or judgment if they don't reach the *'level'* people expect them to be at.

My goal, through youth empowerment, is to help all people (not only youngsters) understand the true value and meaning of knowing God for themselves. If He is everything to us, including our friend, why can't we question Him? Those who know me know I want to know 'why.' The 'why' needs to make sense to me, or I need to be convicted even if I don't understand it. As a result, I have hardened my heart to the cycles and societal norms relating to tradition and the world. We cannot continue to make the world happy by trying to please everyone while neglecting our lives, mental health, and happiness, but we can remain respectful. Religion is not as important as people make it out to be. It is just what they grew up in and are used to, and they find it hard to break away from it; it is like a bad habit. Until we accept that we take different routes to get to our destiny and our purpose, we will continue to go in cycles. The way society is, we have to break away from certain norms and jump into what our hearts desire. You are not wrong for wanting what you want; you desire and experience things that some people will never comprehend. Why? You are unique in every way possible. Find your peace, purpose, destiny, and calling: FIND YOU!

I want you to take a moment and write down at least three things you grew up being told to believe in, but it doesn't

UNLEARNING

resonate with you the more you mature, and then challenge yourself to unlearn those three things day by day and see how you can make a change in your life, this time, for YOU! Then come back to this section and jot down how you managed to make that change.

_____

_____

_____

_____

_____

_____

_____

_____

_____

_____

_____

_____

_____

_____

_____

_____

CHAPTER THREE

CULTIVATING A CULTURE OF ACCEPTANCE

Constantly being told how I should act, talk, think, and walk. Sensing dictation instead of mentorship because I felt I had to learn who I was through other people. Draining myself and my emotions over things I could not control sent me back into a place of despair that I never thought I would revisit. I thought once I saw the signs, I would nip it in the bud before it reached its previous state or worse. What am I talking about? Depression. I underestimated how serious mental health was; I never understood how deeply one could sink once you are caught in a bad place.

I was always told that the young people were waiting for me to fulfil my purpose and destiny so I could help them. So, I had to ensure I stayed in alignment with the Word of God. Whew, the pressure was unbelievable! The guilt was just as heavy if I ever slipped up. Eventually, I realized how depressed I was becoming. I was back at square one. I noticed the cycle, identified the cause, and nipped it in the bud. There is a thin line between helping others and pouring into them while you are wrecking yourself because you don't know when to say no or take a break.

The relentless effort to please society and meet the expectations of others to the point where you lose yourself and the vision of what you want for yourself is daunting. You can lose who YOU want to become because someone told you what would suit you more and what is better or more manageable for you. Admittedly, people may sometimes see things in you that you have yet to discover for yourself, but this doesn't mean you don't know the power, strength, and fight in you. It only means the time is yet to come for you to take on that phase.

I remember and know what it feels like to think I am not or will never be good enough for anyone or anything. However, with my state of mind then, my unyielding determination to get what I wanted felt like my only escape from a dark, lonely, stagnant place. I have always told myself I can have it if it exists because I get whatever I set my mind to. People always told me that no one could change my mind once I made up my mind about what I wanted to do. They were right, but this can be both good and bad. So, I have learned to be less stubborn; if someone tells me I am falling into a ditch, I will take heed, analyze the situation thoroughly, and do what is best. I have always believed that while someone can tell you or me to do something, we cannot blame them if it goes wrong because we could have chosen to accept or reject the suggestion. You lose focus on yourself when you cannot accept things for what they are and are more concerned about what you need to do to be accepted in a particular space. Regardless of your choice, it won't make you more relevant or less important. Whatever you choose to do is all up to you, and all effects and consequences, both good and bad, will reflect not just how you handled the situation but also your character. I accepted that I wasn't placed on this earth to serve every young person. I collaborate with those whose paths align with my story, journey, and purpose. By doing so, I can better empower them to pursue their long-held dreams.

Who said you can't dream anymore because it would not be for you if God didn't place the idea in your mind? Doesn't He grant the desires of our hearts? As long as it is pure, and He knows it is within your capabilities, He will give it to you and journey with you as you mature. Think of it like your parents, siblings, or close friends—they would assist with your studies to ensure you are educated enough to take on the world during adulthood and do this thing called life all on your own. Nothing new is happening in this world; it has all happened before. This is just a different approach.

Stop taking it personally when someone says you are not good enough. Everybody has their crowd, target, life, experiences, cycles, and ups and downs that they must confront. No one can tell you that you will not make it or be unable to do something you have always wanted to do. There is always another way. Accept your destiny and truth. Accept who you see yourself as and not what anyone tells you to become, whether personally, professionally or otherwise. Stepping outside our comfort zones can be a hard pill to swallow. We have been conditioned by what we grew up on, heard, saw, and felt, and breaking away from these habits can be difficult. However, you must learn how to break free from these limitations to move to that unstoppable level in your life. When I say unstoppable, it doesn't mean there won't be times when you may become frustrated and not feel like it. You may want to quit, but there will also be moments that remind you that you are stronger than you think. We can usually feel it, but sometimes, we are not motivated enough to push past that fear because of the pressure of stepping out into something new. Fear – isn't it a huge factor in some of the things you want to do or say, things you haven't done yet because you are afraid to fail and disappoint people who had dreams and plans set out for YOUR future? You have the power to change that narrative and live a life pleasing to you and God Himself. We cannot please the masses: stop, think, and act accordingly.

What is something you have always felt insecure about or felt like no matter what you do, you cannot change, and it is a part of you? This can be anything. Maybe something you are passionate about and told you should take a different path but you know where your heart is, and that is what you will pursue no matter what? Write that down and explain how you think it has or will affect the people around you, but also write down why you believe it would affect you more negatively if you do not live and/or pursue what your heart is yearning for. And how you can overcome this if you haven't done so yet.

CHAPTER FOUR

NAVIGATING LIFE ON YOUR OWN TERMS

I knew I had an entrepreneurial mindset from the age of seventeen. That is why, by then, I had already started three businesses; two failed, and the present one is now growing. I didn't see myself living off my parents forever. I always wanted to have money without asking when I needed something or wanted to go somewhere. I tried nonstop to find a business that would bring me a steady income after I finished high school, but I couldn't find one. My only issue was that I had the vision but lacked the strategy to solidify my plans and make them work. I always acted on 'having a good feeling about this' and just did it.

Though I had a few failed attempts, it taught me determination, and each mistake had its unique lesson. I had no money management skills; after selling a product or offering a service, I didn't invest the profit I made, which caused the businesses to suffer. I didn't understand that start-up/new business ventures required sacrifice, consistency, and accountability. I thought that as soon as I made a profit, I should go and buy whatever I wanted. This contributed to a sense of independence and my desire to boldly call myself an entrepreneur. I didn't pour back into my businesses and seek the necessary tools and guidance I needed because I always felt like doing it my way was good enough. I thought I didn't have to learn anyone's strategy because, at the time, mine was working well enough. I had forgotten that there are levels to success.

Entrepreneurship and wanting to be our own boss is a dream many wish they could have because of the perceived freedom it comes with. However, not everyone has the consistency or patience to do what it takes to be successful as an entrepreneur because they become demotivated as soon as something goes wrong. Did you know that being an entrepreneur doesn't mean you can't work for someone else? You can do both. What makes you think you have to limit yourself? This is especially true when your business is just a start-up; you may need another income stream to accommodate and sustain it so you can reinvest until it reaches its full potential.

Don't let societal norms fool you and tell you that you cannot classify yourself as an entrepreneur if you work for others. Having the title may sound and look fancy when introduced in a space, but having substance for an impact is necessary because you cannot pour from an empty vessel. Do your research, set a goal, stay focused, and initiate. Learn from people in the space you want to be in and utilize social media.

There are many things to learn about, such as using Google, YouTube, and TikTok. You have a wealth of information at your disposal; the key is to be determined to dig and find the right space to be in and the right people to talk to. You CAN do it!

Independence is a great way to step into adulthood, fostering accountability and learning self-control. The aim is to maintain an open mindset so that even when something doesn't work out, you take a break and try something new. You can make it work if you want to; the only thing hindering you is you and your lack of self-discipline.

CHAPTER FIVE

THRIVING INTO THE UNKNOWN

I migrated! To this day, I still find it hard to accept that I left Jamaica, the place where I grew up and spent most of my life outside of my home country. I left my family behind. I knew how difficult that transition would have been for me, but I also knew it was the only option because I couldn't survive in Jamaica. I felt like every turn I made was just another roadblock, and all I could think about while I was in Jamaica was how much easier life would have been if I were in America.

What troubled me and broke me the most was leaving the people I loved behind. Even though I had the opportunity to visit them at any given time, I knew it wouldn't be the same. I remember having mental breakdowns; I would drive to my friend's house and cry in their laps as they hugged me and gave me comfort. Otherwise, I spoke to my mother and expressed my frustration, and she would squeeze me and tell me everything would be alright. I love my mommy with every fiber of my being; I have been so attached to her since childhood. Yes, I am a momma's boy. Everywhere I go, she goes, and vice versa. I miss that, and I miss her; family means so much to me.

I discovered that my primary love languages are physical touch and quality time. Being around the people I love or hearing from them can instantly turn a bad day into a refreshing one. I didn't have that physical support anymore, and travelling miles away from everyone and everything I knew broke me more than anyone could imagine. There were days I wanted to pack my bags, leave, and return to Jamaica because I felt a void and knew what I was missing.

The transition was so sudden that I didn't even expect it. My life took a turn in January 2021, when I felt like there was nothing left for me to do, having tried all without success. November 2021 marked my return to Jamaica, and within the same week, guess what? I bought my first car. Me! A car owner? At twenty-one? Yeah! No one knew except my close friends and family and those who saw me around. I felt like my life was coming together. I didn't have any needs or wants because—remember those crazy hours I worked? Well, I believed I made enough money to last until I was ready to leave for the next work season. Since 2019, some people knew I would leave Jamaica in April for work and return to Jamaica in the summer. I had goals, and I made sure they happened. I worked three jobs! I have never worked that hard in my life, but, as they often do, things fell apart, leaving me in a predicament.

Raheen R. Frith

While working and sending money to my account in Jamaica, there was miscommunication about over Three Hundred Thousand Jamaican Dollars, which had not yet been deposited. This was months after the fact, so I decided to deal with it when I returned to Jamaica. For weeks, I searched for answers concerning my money until, one day, I checked my bank statement. The money was already in my account; it was just miscalculated—an oversight. I was stunned. I had already bought my car, and the leftover money was only enough to cover all the necessary paperwork to make sure the vehicle was fit to drive.

Now, I was left blank financially. I had no plan B. The money that was miscalculated was intended to be used for some bulk designs for my clothing brand and some intense marketing and promotion to build the business and make it a great source of income. Instead, immediately after the purchase, I struggled to make ends meet. My options had disappeared into thin air. I was back at square one, only with a car; I was broke. The car insurance needed to be paid, and the car needed to be maintained. Life's necessities needed to be taken care of, so I fought to find a way out. Then came February. I decided that now was the time to consider leaving Jamaica for good. The roadblocks were popping up frequently. I would have been partially fine if it hadn't been so difficult to get a job in Jamaica.

March 2021 came, and I thought about leaving earlier to avoid a few debts. I stayed. I was forced to sell my iPhone 12 Pro Max. Thankfully, the resale value in Jamaica was high, and I managed to cover 95% of my bills with the proceeds. I also had to sell my laptop, professional camera, and printer, which I had bought for business. These were the most valuable things I owned. Eventually, I had nothing at all. That was my breaking point. Selling the car wasn't an option; my family needed a car. Eventually, I decided to leave it with them...no questions asked.

Those who saw me with the car always thought I had it all together. Others passed very distasteful remarks, including someone very close to me in the past. There was so much going on for me in a short time, and to them, it looked unbelievable. How could it be—I was so young. I had all those things happening for me, including a feature in the Jamaica Gleaner, thanks to my publisher, Crystal Daye, getting my first television interview, and starting a clothing line that seemed to have taken off. I bought a car and travelled to at least three different countries in a few months; it seemed like a lot to some, so where did I get all that money to do all that? Right? That former friend said that I joined a cult to gain riches. Others said I had a sugar momma; there were just so many things being said. These people didn't know that I usually worked seven consecutive days, three jobs, from seven o'clock in the morning to ten o'clock at night. The sources of the accusations were unexpected, but I certainly did not let it bother me.

All that time, I was going through my phase of unlearning numerous things, and I had made a conscious decision to be in a better place. I contacted my job and told them I wanted to start working earlier than usual, and they didn't hesitate to have me back. I just needed to get a date. I got the ticket money within two weeks and booked my ticket for the following week. I didn't have enough time to say my goodbyes because there were so many things to do before I travelled, including renewing my passport. Thanks to the US embassy for making everything happen for me so soon. I stepped out in faith and booked the plane ticket even before I got back my passport, which was returned to me mere days before my departure.

I was overwhelmed, so I constantly had anxiety attacks about starting a new life all by myself. The transition was one of the hardest things I had ever done, but I knew it was what I needed to do, not just for me but to help my family as well. An extra helping hand eased the burden; as usual, just being able to help made me so happy. I always looked forward to this privilege.

Change is hard. Sometimes, we won't see its value until we fully calm our minds and that it is what is needed, even when we don't want to accept it. I learned that stepping out of my comfort zone and doing the unfamiliar motivates and pushes me harder to make something happen. I work, focus, and stay true to myself. I try to prioritize my mental health now more than anything because I have been going through a lot. Now, more than ever, I am not afraid to admit this and be open to the changes and struggles I have gone through or am going through. Why? I know that as soon as I overcome them, they will be my greatest strengths and testimonies to help someone and to guide them through their rough phase. Transparency has given me so much peace of mind and has allowed me to find what I am destined for and target who I am called to lead without pressure or judgment.

Change is necessary and inevitable. There is nothing wrong with you for outgrowing thoughts, past beliefs, and dreams you once held dear. The more you understand life and what aligns with your needs, the more you learn to evolve and be true to yourself and your calling. Sometimes, we know we desperately need to leave a place we are accustomed to, and even when it hurts us and creates a toxic space, we find it difficult to leave it behind. Usually, those are the things that hold us back from reaching our full potential. Find your 'WHY,' and you will understand what you need for yourself. Remember, this is on your terms, and there is always room for improvement. Just believe in yourself no matter what. You got this, we got this!

What stood out to you the most? What lesson did you learn, and how can you improve and break free from outdated beliefs and societal norms? Let this section now become a personal moment to reflect and jot down what you will be taking control of from now on and how you will become an even better version of yourself.

_____

_____

_____

ABOUT THE AUTHOR

Raheen Frith is a dynamic force to be reckoned with. At just twenty-one years old, his debut book, UNLOCK: The Journey to Purpose, quickly became a best-seller and claimed the third spot in its category in 2020. But his talents extend far beyond the realm of writing. Raheen is also a passionate youth philanthropist, dedicated dancer, adventurous traveler, and freelance model. His boundless creativity and zest for life infuse every aspect of his work making him a true inspiration to his readers and beyond.

www.ingramcontent.com/pod-product-compliance
Lightning Source LLC
Chambersburg PA
CBHW060858050426
42453CB00008B/1007